The Christmas Visitors by Karel Hayes

To John and Lesley
May all your Christmases be merry!

ISBN 978-1-60893-248-1

Printed in the United States

Down East Books

A member of the Rowman & Littlefield Publishing Group

4501 Forbes Boulevard, Suite 200 • Lanham, Maryland 20706

www.downeastbooks.com

Distributed by

NATIONAL BOOK NETWORK

1-800-462-6420

The summer visitors have gone home

and the winter visitors

are left behind.

So sad it is,

but not for everyone.

Oh, why not

pack the presents,

take the bags;

and take a ride on a train

to a far away favorite place.

snowing hard and need a ride;

Christmas trees all sold out, and turkey, too,

make it hard

to celebrate.

Merry holidays,

twinkling lights,

and starlit skies;

all go round and round

  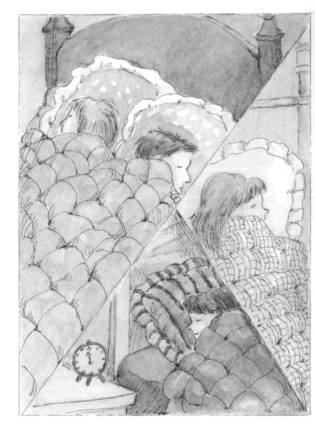

and off to bed.

Surprise,

surprise,

and Christmas cheer

make a Happy New Year

for everyone.